Baby's bathtime

Fiona Watt

pictures by Rachel Wells

managing designer: Mary Cartwright   series editor: Jenny Tyler

First published in 1998, Usborne Publishing Ltd, Usborne House, 83-85 Saffron Hill, London, EC1N 8RT. www.usborne.com © 1998 Usborne Publishing Ltd.
The name Usborne and the device ⊕ are Trademarks of Usborne Publishing Ltd. All rights reserved. No part of this publication may be reproduced,
stored in a retrieval system or transmitted in any form or by any means, electronic, mechanical, photocopying, recording, or otherwise, without
previous permission of the publisher. First published in America 1999. Printed in Belgium.

What a mess!
It's time for a bath.

Off with my clothes.

I can pull off my socks.

I have fun with all my toys.
Look out Fido!

I splash and splash.

I have my hair washed.

It makes it stick up.

I get dried in a big fluffy towel.

Toothpaste time.

Don't do that, Fido!

Time for bed.
Night night.